W9-AWW-863

THE SIGN PAINTER'S SECRET

The Story of a Revolutionary Girl

Annie Laurie MacDougal

THE SIGN PAINTER'S SECRET

The Story of a Revolutionary Girl

BY DOROTHY AND THOMAS HOOBLER

AND CAREY-GREENBERG ASSOCIATES

PICTURES BY DONNA AYERS

KINGSWAY
CHRISTIAN
SCHOOL
LIBRARY

SILVER BURDETT PRESS

Copyright © 1991 by
Carey-Greenberg Associates
Illustrations © 1991 by
Donna Ayers

All rights reserved including
the right of reproduction in
whole or in part in any form.

Published by Silver Burdett Press, Inc.,
a division of Simon & Schuster, Inc.,
Prentice Hall Bldg.,
Englewood Cliffs, NJ 07632

Designed by Leslie Bauman

Illustrations on pages 49, 51, and 52
by Leslie Dunlap

Manufactured in the
United States of America

10 9 8 7 6 5 4

**Library of Congress Cataloging-
in-Publication Data**

Hoobler, Dorothy.
The sign painter's secret :
the story of a revolutionary girl /
by Dorothy and Thomas Hoobler
and Carey-Greenberg Associates.
p.   cm.—(Her story)
Summary: When the Redcoats occupy her
house in Philadelphia, young Annie
MacDougal finds a way to help General
Washington's troops at Valley Forge.
ISBN 0-382-24143-6 (lib. bdg.)—ISBN 0-382-24150-9
ISBN 0-382-24345-5 (pbk.)
1. United States—History—Revolution,
1775–1783—Juvenile fiction.
[1. United States—History—Revolution,
1775–1783—Fiction. 2. Spies—Fiction.]
I. Hoobler, Thomas. II. Carey-Greenberg
Associates. III. Title. IV. Series.
PZ7.H76227Si   1991
[Fic]—dc20   90-37353   CIP   AC

CONTENTS

CHAPTER ONE

The Redcoats Move In

''REDCOATS!'' Annie Laurie MacDougal whispered to herself. She clenched her fists as she watched the rows of British soldiers march down Market Street. All that summer of 1777 they had been fighting General Washington's army. And now they had captured Philadelphia! Annie fought back her tears.

Seeing the Redcoats made Annie wonder what had happened to her older brother, Rob. He was fighting in the Revolutionary army, but they had not received a letter from him in months. At night Annie had heard her mother pacing the floor of her bedroom, unable to sleep. Though she tried to reassure her children that they would hear from Rob soon, Annie knew she was as worried as they were.

Her family members were strong supporters of the cause of independence. A month ago, Annie's father had gone away too. A wealthy cloth merchant, he had given his stock to make uniforms for Washington's army. But the army also needed muskets and food and cannons. Mr. MacDougal had left for Charleston to try to raise money for the Revolution.

"It's better that your father is gone," Annie's mother had told her yesterday. "If the British take the city, they will arrest anyone suspected of helping the Revolution. Now he'll be safe." Annie hoped that was true. When the Revolution began, she had been glad. It was exciting to think that the colonists would have their own country. She thought the war would be all over in a few weeks. She hadn't known it would split up her family. Sometimes she even wished—

Suddenly a cheer rang out from the crowd of people watching the British troops. Annie stood on tiptoe, but she couldn't see over their heads. She heard shouts, and the crowd moved forward, pushing her along.

She looked around, struggling to stay on her feet. Where was Brian? Her eight-year-old brother had come with her to see the British. Their mother had told Annie to watch out for him, and now he was gone! "Brian! Brian!" she called. She pulled at the sleeve of a woman in the crowd. "What's happening?"

"Some boy threw a stone at the Redcoats," the woman said. "They're chasing him!" someone else called.

Oh no! Annie thought. It would be just like Brian, the little hothead, to do that. He and his friends used wooden broomsticks as muskets and swords, pretending they were fighting the British. She called his name again.

"Up here!" Annie heard Brian's voice, and she looked up. Brian had climbed to the top of some crates that stood outside a candle maker's shop. "They didn't catch him!" Brian yelled.

With relief, Annie hauled him down and pulled him away from the crowd. On the way home he told her excitedly about seeing the boy throw the stone.

"The soldiers might have killed him," Annie said.

"Remember what Rob said?" Brian asked. "You must be ready to fight for freedom."

Annie bit her lip. She remembered Rob saying that, and it made her feel proud. If only she'd

had a stone, she might have thrown it herself. But she didn't tell Brian that.

When they reached their house, Annie tried not to look at their father's shop next door, with the sign MacDougal Fine Cloth. Shutters were drawn across the windows, and the shop was empty. She had loved to go there and feel the different kinds of cloth—brocade, silk, muslin, and wool. Bolts of them were displayed along the walls, some dyed in beautiful colors and others decorated with prints or embroidery. Would it ever be open again?

Their large brick house seemed empty and dark too. Before the war it was always full of people. Friends and merchants from other cities came to visit. At parties she and Brian sat in the children's corner of the ballroom, watching the dancers swirl around in their silk suits and dresses.

Now, visitors were rare. The MacDougals had let their servants go, for it was too expensive to keep them. Most of the doors were kept closed in summer so that the heat from the big kitchen fireplace would not spread through the house. She and Brian rushed back there, drawn by the smell of mutton soup.

"How did the British look?" their mother

asked. She was standing at the great brick fireplace that was taller than she was. Hanging on the wall were small pots and iron kitchen tools. The kitchen was always hot, making it a good place in the winter, but now Annie broke into a sweat as soon as she entered. Flies swarmed through the open windows.

Mother ladled soup from the "spider," a large kettle with three legs that sat right on top of the hot coals in the fireplace. Annie carried the steaming bowls to the heavy wooden table in the cook's room next to the kitchen. When their father was home, they always ate their meals in the dining room, but it was easier for the three of them to eat here.

Annie was hungry, but she ate slowly, saving the small scraps of mutton for last. She knew that food was scarce, and they had to make the soup do for supper as well. Some families didn't even have mutton, for sheep were now more valuable for their wool than for meat. Before the war most of the colonies' wool had come from Britain. Now the colonists had to make their own homespun cloth.

Brian was more interested in talking than eating. He excitedly told their mother about the boy who threw the stone at the British. Mother frowned. "That was a foolish thing to do," she said. "It served no purpose, and the soldiers might have hurt him."

"Foolish!" Brian said. "We've got to fight the British!"

"They won't be defeated with stones, Brian," Mother said.

Suddenly they heard the thump-thump of the brass knocker on the front door. Annie and Brian ran to the parlor and peeped through the curtains. On the windowsill was a "busybody," a small mirror that let them see who was at the door.

They looked at each other in alarm. It was a British officer!

"Don't open it!" Brian said when their mother approached. "It's a Redcoat!"

But Mother calmly opened the door. Brian and Annie peeped at him from behind her hoop skirt.

"Mrs. MacDougal?" the officer asked.

Mother nodded.

The officer held out a piece of paper. "I have orders from General Howe to examine your house."

Mother let him inside. Annie watched him curiously. He was polite, but explained that the British needed places for their troops to stay. "You have a large house," he said, looking through the door that led to the ballroom. "How many people are living here?"

"Just the three of us," Mother said. Annie held her breath, wondering if the officer would ask where their father was.

Instead, he seemed pleased with the answer. "How many of King George's officers can you accommodate?"

"We have no servants," Mother said, "and little enough food for ourselves."

"We will provide food," the officer said. "I think you may find that a few extra guests will be no trouble."

And that was that. In the days that followed, five British officers moved into the MacDougal house. Annie and Brian had to move their clothing up to the servants' bedrooms on the third floor. Mother slept up there too.

Mother had to serve as the British officers' cook and maid, making up their rooms and preparing their meals. They ate quite a lot, though it was true that butchers and grocers delivered more than enough. And it was better food than the MacDougals had eaten since the war began. But the worst part was that Mother seemed quite calm, even cheerful, about all this.

Brian complained bitterly. "At least we could

try to poison their food," he said. But Mother only replied, "Remember what Benjamin Franklin said. 'Little strokes may fell great oaks.'"

"What does that mean?" Brian said. But Mother only smiled. Annie thought about it. Mother meant that they could do something to hurt the British. But what?

CHAPTER TWO

The Secret Messenger

WEEKS WENT BY, and it seemed as if the British would stay forever. It was November now, and they seemed content to stay in Philadelphia all winter. Rumors swept the city that General Washington's army was nearby. But those who hoped he would recapture the city were disappointed.

Meanwhile, Brian was fighting his own little wars. One day he came home with cuts and bruises on his face and hands. Annie got some water from the well and washed Brian's face. But she couldn't soothe his feelings. "He called me a Tory!" Brian sobbed. "My best friend, Andrew! I hate him!"

"You know we're not Tories, Brian." Tories were the people of the colonies who favored the British side. They wanted the King of England to go on ruling America. In 1776 most of the Tories in Philadelphia had been run out of the city.

But now, with the British in control of Philadelphia, many of them returned. They received the good food and clothing that British ships unloaded on the docks along the Delaware River. Tories went to the grand parties at the houses where British officers were staying.

That was why Brian's friend had called him a Tory. The MacDougal house had become a nightly gathering place for many of the British officers.

"At least we have good food," Annie said to Brian, "even if it is to feed the British officers."

"That's the worst part of it," he said. "Nobody but the Tories has beef and lamb and so much to eat. I'm never going to eat again."

Annie left him and went downstairs. In mid-afternoon there were no British at home. Her mother was in the kitchen making applesauce.

"Lend a hand, Annie," Mother said.

"Brian got in another fight," Annie said as she began to cut the cores out of the apples.

Mother shook her head. "Temper," she said. "Like his father."

"Someone called him a Tory," Annie said.

Mother grated some nutmeg and put it into the big kettle with the apples. Annie couldn't understand how calm her mother was. She acted as if it didn't matter that the British made her stay up all night serving them food and drink!

Mother wiped her hands and took an envelope from her apron pocket. Annie saw that it was sealed with wax. "I'll talk with Brian," she said. "Meanwhile, I want you to run an errand. You know how to find Matthew Brent's shop on Arch Street?"

Annie nodded. "He has a beautiful sign outside the shop. What do you need from him?" Annie asked.

"Don't worry about that. Put the envelope inside your dress. Be careful you don't attract attention to yourself or show it to anyone. You must give it only to Mr. Brent himself."

Annie put on her bonnet and coat, wondering about the strange errand. Mr. Brent was a sign painter. He had made the sign that hung outside Father's shop. Did Mother want him to change it now? Or perhaps take it down and store it for safekeeping?

She left the house and made her way through the busy city. It was market day, and all along Market Street people were selling food. Wagons and stalls displayed apples and pears, vegetables of all kinds, and fresh fish and meat. In the crowded streets she passed Quakers with broad black hats, men in bright silk suits, and others in drab work clothes. Free Negroes and red-coated soldiers added to the varied mix of people. She heard the sounds of French and German, as well as English.

Turning into Arch Street, she saw three boys laughing and rolling hoops down the street. They stopped and glared at three British soldiers coming out of a tavern. The soldiers shouted at them, and the boys ran. As the soldiers passed Annie, she turned her eyes downward, remembering her mother's warning.

When they had gone, she entered the little shop with the sign of an artist's brush and palette. It showed that Mr. Brent was an artist who painted whatever people wanted. Though he did portraits and landscapes, he was best known for his signs for shops.

Inside, the air was heavy with the smell of turpentine and paint. In a corner of the room, a young apprentice was working on a sign. Annie walked over to look. Before the war she had taken drawing lessons. But she hadn't done anything with real paint.

The sign bore the words *The King's Tavern*. Above them was a half-finished portrait of King George III. She frowned. Another Tory working for the British. Then she caught herself. That was what people thought of her family too.

"Annie MacDougal," a voice said. "You've grown." Mr. Brent had stepped from behind a curtained doorway that led to another room. He was a small man, middle-aged and bald, but Annie's eyes were drawn to his long, slender hands. They moved with the grace of swans.

She reached under her coat and drew out the letter. "My mother sent this." Almost before she knew it, he reached out and slid it from her hand. He opened the envelope and scanned the note quickly. It seemed to please him.

Mr. Brent glanced at his apprentice, who was still at work on the sign. "Francis," he said. "You have a pupil. Teach Miss MacDougal how to draw. I must go out." He looked at Annie. "Wait here until I return."

Francis seemed as surprised as Annie was. He was about twenty, the same age as Rob. He wore a smock that was stained with paint, and he looked slightly annoyed at having his work interrupted. "Can you paint?" he said.

"Not as well as you," she said. That seemed to

please him. "Let's start with something simple then. I'll show you how to make a silhouette," he said.

He drew the curtains over the front windows, making the shop quite dark. Then he lit a single candle and set it on a small table near the wall. Drawing up a chair, he asked her to sit, and then used a tack to attach a sheet of drawing paper to the wall. After he adjusted the candle, she could see the shadow of her head and shoulders on the paper. "You'll have to sit still now," he said.

Rapidly, he outlined with a charcoal stick the shadow her head made on the paper. He took the paper down. "Fill it in with lampblack," he said. "Try to stay within the outline. You'll learn to keep your hand steady."

He opened the curtains and went back to his work. Annie was only half-finished when Mr. Brent returned. He looked at the silhouette. "Very good," he said. "Take it home now and bring it back when you've finished. Tell your mother that I said you have done very well."

Annie made her way back home, puzzled. She showed the silhouette to her mother and repeated Mr. Brent's message. Mother smiled. "Mr. Brent thinks you show promise. I'd like you to take more lessons."

When Annie finished the silhouette, Mother

sent her back to Mr. Brent's shop with another message. Annie began to go there two or three times a week. Francis showed her how to mix watercolors, and she painted a few simple landscapes.

But Mr. Brent hardly seemed to look at her work. He seemed more interested in the notes Mother wrote. And Mother continued to warn Annie not to show them to anyone but Mr. Brent himself.

It all seemed strange. Why had Mother suddenly decided to send her for art lessons? Why was it such a secret?

Maybe her mother was using the art lessons to keep Annie out of the house. Life with the British officers was getting worse and worse. They came and went at all hours, and mother spent most nights downstairs serving them. Often, Annie and Brian could not sleep because of the sounds of shouts and laughter that echoed through the house.

Annie decided she must speak to her mother. That night she waited until the house was finally quiet and tiptoed down the hallway to Mother's bedroom.

When she opened the door, she saw Mother writing a letter by the dim light of a candle. Mother quickly covered it with a piece of blot-

ting paper. She turned her head and seemed relieved that it was Annie.

"Why are you up so late, dear?" Mother asked.

Annie sat on the bed. "Mother, we've got to do
something about the British."

"What would you have us do, Annie?" Mother
had gone back to her writing. It annoyed Annie.

"Can't we go away? To Charleston? To find
Father?"

"What if he returned and we weren't here?
How would he know where we'd gone?"

"Mother, if he did come back . . . what would
he think to find we're helping the British? How
can you smile at them so when Rob is fighting
them?"

Finally, Mother put down her quill pen. She
came and held Annie tightly. "Annie, you mustn't
speak of your father and brother, of what they're
doing. The British mustn't suspect."

"Why not? I don't care what they'd do to us. I
don't want to be a Tory. I want to do something."

Mother patted her head. "We are doing something, Annie. I thought it was best if you didn't
know, but you're taking a great risk. Those messages that you take to Mr. Brent—he sends them
on to General Washington."

Annie's eyes widened. "But why? What is in
them?"

"Washington's men are camped at Valley Forge, only twenty miles away. They are almost too weak to fight. If the British decide to attack, Washington must know about it as soon as possible. You understand?"

"Yes, but how do you . . . Oh! You listen to the British!"

Mother smiled. "You're very clever, Annie. Yes, they talk freely in front of me. To them I'm just a servant. Indeed, General Howe himself was here two nights ago. He thinks we are Tories, and so we must pretend to be."

"But we're spies!" Annie's eyes flashed.

Mother put her finger on Annie's lips. "Yes. But spies never talk about their work. What we're doing is very dangerous, Annie. I worry about you all the time you're gone."

Mother paused. "I don't know whether it is right to send you. But if I went myself it would only cause suspicion. And"—Mother smiled—"I could not send Brian."

"He could never keep a secret," Annie agreed.

Annie went back to bed, but she could not sleep. She didn't worry about the danger. That didn't bother her. But it was so exciting to think that she was a spy! If only there were someone she could tell. But she reminded herself—spies never talk.

CHAPTER THREE

Escape!

FEBRUARY had been a cold month. Snow covered the streets, and the horses packed it down hard. A rare warm day only melted it a little, and it froze into ice the next night, making walking even more difficult. Yet once or twice a week, Annie continued her "art lessons" at Mr. Brent's shop. She was proud now that she knew she was a spy.

But there was bad news. Rumors swept the city that Washington's army was starving. The British officers in Annie's house cheered the news that deserters from the rebel army had begun to stumble into the city. "These colonials don't have the stomach for a real fight," Annie heard the officers say.

Today, Annie's mother had seemed especially excited when she gave her the message for Mr. Brent. "Take good care," she told Annie. "This may be the last message you'll have to carry."

Annie wrapped her heavy blue woolen cloak around her and stepped into the icy air. The streets were nearly empty, and she felt as if eyes were watching her from the windows of the houses along the way.

But as she drew near to Arch Street, she heard a commotion. As she turned the corner, she saw a troop of red-coated soldiers. She stifled a cry as she saw they were outside the sign painter's shop. A crowd of people had gathered to watch, and Annie cautiously slipped closer.

Most of the crowd were Tories, for they were talking excitedly about catching a rebel. "I hear they've found gunpowder in his storeroom," one of them said. "Muskets too. Ready to kill all of us loyalists in our beds," said another.

Suddenly the door of the shop swung open and two soldiers came out, dragging a man between them. It was Mr. Brent! The crowd shouted angrily and surged forward. The other soldiers waved their muskets, with bayonets attached. "Keep back now," they told the crowd. "We're taking him to prison."

"Hang him!" someone shouted. A British sergeant turned and nodded. "Likely we will," he said. "He's a spy." Annie started to touch her cloak pocket where she carried the message, but she caught herself. Some of the crowd threw stones at the shop windows. Annie turned as slowly as she could and walked the other way, hearing the noise of breaking glass behind her.

At home Mother was alarmed by the story Annie told. "Did anyone question you?" Mother asked. "Notice you?"

"No," Annie said. "I'm sure of it. I was just part of the crowd."

Mother thought for a minute. "Mr. Brent will not give us away."

"Will they really hang him?" Annie asked. "When they caught a family watching British boats on the river one night, they burned their house down."

"They may," Mother said. "But sometimes they only jail people they suspect of being rebels."

"Can't we do something to help him?"

Mother shook her head. "Everyone who helps knows the risk he takes. Just as you and I have, Annie. But it's a shame we couldn't send this message. It's a very important one." She took the letter from Annie and thrust it into the kitchen fire, stirring the ashes to make sure nothing was left.

"What was the message?" asked Annie.

"Something I heard when one of General Howe's staff was here. Howe has decided to keep his army in Philadelphia until the winter's over. Washington is safe from attack until spring."

"That's good news!" Annie said.

"Yes, and it would raise the spirits of Washington's men. It might help him to keep them together."

That night Annie tossed and turned in her bed. She worried about Mr. Brent and about her brother Rob, who might be with Washington. But most of all, she worried about the important message that now would never get to Washington.

Unless . . . someone took a risk. By the time the sun came up, she had decided what she must do.

After Mother served the British officers their breakfast, she asked Annie and Brian to go to the market. Ashamed of herself for lying, Annie said that her throat was sore and she felt feverish. Mother sent her to bed, and she and Brian left. The house was empty.

Quickly, Annie searched through an old trunk for some of Rob's old clothes that would fit her. The boots were loose, but she put on an extra pair of cotton stockings under them. She would need boots, for she was going to ride on horseback. She pinned her hair up and tucked it inside a three-cornered hat. Looking in the hall mirror, she almost giggled. She tried to ignore the fact that her heart was pounding.

In the stable behind the house, she saddled old Fred, the last horse they had. Rob had taken their best horse when he joined the army, and their father had ridden the other one to Charleston. Annie patted Fred's neck and stroked his ears as she fed him a bagful of oats. "Eat up, Fred," she said. "We've got a long ride ahead."

At the last minute, Annie decided that her mother would be too worried if she didn't know what Annie was doing. Of course, she thought, Mother would worry if she *did* know, but that couldn't be helped. In case a British officer found it, she simply left a note saying, "The new painting is being delivered."

In a way it was a good thing that Fred was such an old horse. As he clip-clopped slowly along the icy streets, no one gave them a second glance. Annie tried not to look as if she were in any hurry.

By the time she came to the outskirts of the city, she heard a church bell striking nine. She saw three British sentries warming their hands around the fire. As they looked up, she reined in old Fred. With a humble look, she pointed to the road that led up the Schuylkill River. One of the sentries waved her on. They were on guard for Washington's soldiers, not for a boy returning to his family's farm.

Annie's relief soon turned to worry. She was on her own now, and she didn't know quite where she was going. Washington's army was at Valley Forge. She knew only that it was near the Schuylkill River. Well, there was the river on her left. All she had to do was follow it.

But soon the road turned into the country-side. All around her were snow-covered fields that had been harvested months before. Once in a while she saw the smoke of a farmhouse, but no one ventured out into the cold. In wartime people had good reason to hide from strangers traveling along the road. Soldiers on both sides sometimes raided farms for food.

Old Fred moved ever more slowly. He kept turning his head to look at Annie. Probably he was even colder than she was and longed for his warm stall. Finally she stopped to give him a rest. She took out the bread and cheese she had brought in a small sack. She wolfed most of it down before realizing that she ought to save some for later.

Fred watched her eat, and she tried to kick some of the snow aside so he could have some grass. But she uncovered only a few frozen brown shoots. She offered Fred a chunk of bread that she had torn off the loaf. He ate it so quickly that she gave him the rest of her bread. Then she remounted him and started on. The sun told her it was already past noon, and she had far to go.

As the afternoon drew on, she saw someone else walking down the road toward her. He looked like a beggar. His filthy coat was in shreds, and he had rags wrapped around his feet. She felt sorry for him, until she drew closer and saw the shifty look he gave her. He stepped in front of old Fred and took the reins. "Where're ye going?" the man said.

Annie swallowed and tried to make her voice sound firm. "To Washington's army," she said.

The man cackled, an ugly sound. "Better hurry," he said. "T'won't be much of an army there before long."

"Is it far?" she asked.

He tossed his head in the direction he had

come from. " 'Bout eight miles." He patted Fred, but the horse shied away from his touch. "I expect you could walk it if you gimme this horse."

"He's *my* horse," Annie said loudly. Suddenly she was afraid and kicked out with her boot, striking the man in the chest. She realized how weak he was when he fell heavily to the ground. She dug her heels into Fred's sides, and he broke into a trot for the first time all day. Annie looked back and saw the man still sitting in the road, cursing her.

Before long, she could see the river on her left again and was relieved. She told herself it wouldn't be much longer. Finally, in the last rays of sunlight, she saw a small village just ahead. A boy about her own age was sitting on a stone wall by the road. She stopped the horse to ask him, "'Do you know where Washington's army is?"

The boy pointed. "Ride over the bridge there," he said. "You'll find them on the other side."

She thanked him and headed for the bridge. "He don't take volunteers as young as you," the boy called. "I already tried."

CHAPTER FOUR

An Army without Shoes

ANNIE RODE across the old wooden bridge and up the hill on the other side. A man stepped out from behind a tree. He looked even worse than the beggar. His shoulders were covered with a tattered blanket. She could hardly believe her eyes when she saw that two old hats were tied to his feet. But then he raised his musket, aiming it straight at her.

"Who goes there?" he said.

She hesitated, not wanting to give her real name. "I'm bringing a message for General Washington," she said.

He looked her over. "You're a mite young."

"That's why I was sent," she said, biting her

tongue at the lie. "I came from Philadelphia."

The city's name seemed to impress him. "Ride on," he said, lowering the musket. "Go to the house on the left, on the edge of camp." He pointed as if she didn't know right from left.

She found the house without difficulty. All around it groups of men sat huddled before small campfires. The air was full of smoke and it stung her eyes.

Annie got off old Fred. As she tied his reins to the post in front of the house, she heard the sound of an approaching horse. Some of the men at the campfires stood and removed their hats. Without thinking, she took hers off too and felt her hair fall down.

Then she saw the mounted rider, whose long black coat covered the flanks of his horse. He glanced at her. He seemed like a giant, the biggest man she had ever seen. "What have we here?" he said.

"I have a message for General Washington," Annie said. "From Philadelphia."

"Well then, you'd better come inside." He called a man to take care of their horses, and led her into the house.

Oil lamps lit up the room. Two men were standing over a table that had a map spread out on it. Ignoring Annie, both of them began to speak at once. They wanted the man in the cloak to settle an argument, but he waved them off.

"Gentlemen," he said. "Here is a messenger, just arrived from Philadelphia."

The men looked at her. One of them was short, heavy, and red-faced. In a heavy German accent he said, "Dis is a liddle gurl." She could tell what he thought of little girls. The other one was red-haired, tall, and looked the same age as her brother Rob. He gave her a wink.

"Where is the message?" the man in the black cloak said.

"It's for General Washington personally," Annie said shyly. The others laughed.

The man swept off his hat, exposing his white wig beneath. Now she saw his face clearly— square, with a broad nose. But his blue eyes twinkled. "I *am* General Washington," he said. He gestured to the others. "This is General von Steuben, who has come from Prussia to train our troops, and the Marquis de Lafayette from France. You may speak freely in front of them."

Annie could hardly catch her breath. She had heard her brother and parents speak of Washington as the greatest man in the colonies. When the colonists rebelled against Britain, everyone agreed he was the man to lead their army.

Quickly, Annie began to explain about her mother listening to the British officers and sending the messages to Mr. Brent. "But the British caught him yesterday."

Washington frowned. "Brent was a valuable man."

"But Mother thought the last message was very important," Annie went on. "General Howe is going to stay in Philadelphia for the rest of the winter."

Washington clapped his hands. The news delighted the others too. "You've done well," Washington said. He turned to General von Steuben. "What do you think of this 'little girl' now?"

Von Steuben clicked his heels and bowed to her. "I made a mistake," he said. "You are an eggzellent zpy!"

"And this excellent spy deserves something to eat," said a woman who had come into the room. She was chubby, with a kind face and brown curly hair.

"My wife, Martha," Washington said. "Here is one more small brave soldier for you to look after."

"I have thousands of them already, including

you," she said with a smile. "Come, dear," she said to Annie. "You look like you're about to drop. We haven't much here, but we share what we have."

When Annie awoke the next morning, she stared at the unfamiliar room. For a second she didn't know where she was. She lay on a straw mattress with no sheets. A rough, itchy blanket covered her. Then she remembered everything that had happened. It seemed like a dream.

She got out of bed, still dressed in the clothes she had arrived in. They felt dirty, and she suddenly missed her mother very much. She splashed some cold water on her face from the bowl that sat on a table by the bed. Feeling a little better, she made her way downstairs.

No one was there but Martha Washington. "You had a good rest," she said cheerfully. "Have one of the fire cakes," she added, gesturing to a stack of flat circles of bread. The cake had almost no taste, but Annie ate it greedily.

"I've been making these all morning for the soldiers who are too sick to cook for themselves," Martha said. "Would you like to help me bring them to the men?"

"Oh yes," said Annie. "Do you know if there's

anyone here named Rob MacDougal? He's my brother."

Martha smiled. "There are thousands of men here, and many named Rob. But maybe we'll see him."

As they walked through the camp, Annie was shocked to see what Washington's army looked like. They had no bright uniforms like the British. Most were barefoot, and she saw with a blush that some had no trousers. Their only protection from the bitter cold were thin blankets wrapped around their bare legs.

All of them looked hungry. Martha stopped by the ones that lay on the ground, too weak to move. She gave them some of the fire cakes. There were other women doing the same thing.

"Some of the other officers' wives have come here as well," Martha explained. "It cheers the men up a little to see us." She added in a whisper, "The ones who are thinking of going home become ashamed when they see that women can bear the hardships too."

Annie saw the tall young man Washington had called the Marquis de Lafayette. He was talking to another man whose back was turned. Something seemed familiar about him. As Annie passed them, she looked at his face.

"Rob?" she said. She wasn't quite sure it really was her brother, for he had changed greatly. His face and body were terribly thin, and he looked much older than she had remembered.

Rob stared back, frozen with disbelief. Then he rushed forward and swooped her into his arms. "Annie!" he shouted. "So you were the spy. Lafayette was just telling me the news."

Annie hugged him. "Oh, Rob, we haven't heard from you in so long. We thought . . . we were afraid—"

"Thought the British had me, eh? They fired a few shots in my direction, but as you can see, they missed. But, Annie, how could Mother have sent you on such a journey?"

Annie hung her head. "She didn't know I was going," she said. "I took Old Fred."

Her brother laughed. She was glad, for then he looked more like the brother she had known.

"You scamp," he said. "I can tell you, though, you brought good news. But we've got to get you back to Philadelphia soon. If Mother was worried about me, imagine what she must be feeling about you."

"I can ride back tomorrow," Annie said.

Rob shook his head. "I won't let you take such

a chance twice. And besides, we can use Old Fred. Horses, clothing, food—we're in desperate need of everything. Lafayette thinks that France will aid us soon. If they do, we cannot lose. But we have to hold out until then."

Martha, who had stood listening to them, interrupted. She said, "I have a way for you to return, Annie. You stay and visit with your brother for a while."

Rob walked with her through the camp. Some of the men in better health were lined up in front of General von Steuben. He was shouting at them in German.

"When he loses his temper, he forgets how to speak English," Rob explained. "He's trying to train them how to march and shoot together, the way the British do. It's hard for them to learn. Most of them are just country boys. If the British attacked us now, we'd be too weak to fight. But thanks to you, we know we have time."

General Washington rode by on his big white horse. Seeing Annie, he gave her a nod. He stopped and spoke to the men von Steuben was training. They seemed to march better when Washington was watching.

"He's holding the men together," Rob said. "Everyone admires him. He's a rich man, you know. He didn't have to join this fight. But if the British win, he'd be the first one they'd hang."

"They won't win!" said Annie.

Rob patted her on the shoulder. "Not as long as the army has people like you behind us."

CHAPTER FIVE

Hooray for President Washington!

LATER THAT DAY, Martha Washington took Annie to a nearby farm. The family there gave her a dress, and the next day took her to Philadelphia on their wagon.

She carried two more messages with her. One was a letter from Rob. The other, Martha Washington had written herself. "This is for your mother," Martha told Annie. "Just to let her know how proud we all are of you." She smiled. "If my daughter had done what you did, I wouldn't know whether to kiss her or tan her."

Annie was worried about that herself. When the farm family bade her farewell at Market Street, she hurried toward her house. Though she had been treated like a heroine at Washington's camp, she wasn't sure how her mother would greet her.

It was lunchtime, and the British officers had returned to the house for their meal. Annie slipped through the alley to the back door. When she went inside, the kitchen was empty. A steaming kettle of beef stew stood on the table. Annie thought of Washington's hungry soldiers and wished she could send them some of this food.

The moment Annie had been dreading came suddenly when her mother brought a stack of empty plates through the door. She stopped and nearly dropped the plates. She set them down carefully, and Annie saw that her hands were shaking.

Then Mother opened her arms and Annie rushed inside them. Mother squeezed her so tightly that Annie could hardly breathe. She had never felt so loved.

"You silly, silly girl," said Mother. "Do you know how much I've worried about you?"

"Oh yes, Mother. I'm sorry, really I am. But I saw Rob, and I've got a letter from him. And Washington! I met him! I stayed in his house and helped Martha Washington, and, oh, here's another letter from her. Read it, please, Mother, before you think I did wrong."

Mother took the letter, turning it over in her hands. "If Martha Washington sent you back with a letter, I know you've done something right. But Annie, promise me now that you'll never do such a thing again."

Annie smiled, because she knew her mother had already forgiven her. "I won't, Mother, but you said yourself it was important. And it was!"

Before her mother could reply, the door to the dining room swung open. It was Brian. "You're back!" he shouted. "I thought you ran away! Mother wouldn't tell me anything, and now I want to know! Where—" They hushed him.

"Annie will tell you where she's been," said Mother. "Here, look, she's brought us a letter from Rob." Brian reached for it eagerly. But Mother shook her finger at him. "Remember, the British think that she's been sick and has stayed upstairs in her room."

She glanced at Annie. "That's what I've told them, and they have no reason to think otherwise." She turned back to Brian. "And it's very important that they never, never know where she has really been."

"If I decide to tell you," Annie said.

"I'll make you tell me," Brian replied.

"Not just yet," said Mother. "The officers are waiting for their lunch."

Annie helped Mother carry out the bowls of stew. One of the officers noticed her. "So," he said. "You're feeling better today? Stay out of the cold weather. It's not healthy for little girls like you."

Annie smiled and curtsied, thinking of General von Steuben. None of these big men thought girls could do anything. They should always use us to be spies, she thought.

After the British had finished lunch and left the house, Annie told Brian and Mother everything that had happened to her. When she described how bad things were at Valley Forge, they looked worried. Annie added, "But they're going to be ready by spring. Everybody believes in Washington."

Mother opened the two letters and read them aloud. Martha Washington had written, "You must be a wonderful mother to have such a brave daughter. I hope you will forgive her, for she only followed your example. You have given not only your son to our army, but risked your own safety as well. With families such as yours, I am sure that we cannot lose the war. General Washington joins me in sending his regards."

Mother set the letter aside. "We will keep it for your father to read," she said. "And someday you can show it to your own children, Annie."

Then she turned to Rob's. "Don't worry about me," he had written. "I think about you often; and someday when the war is over, we'll be together again. I was so proud to hear what all of you were doing for our great cause."

"Except me," Brian grumbled. "Because nobody even told me what was going on."

"Well, now you have something to do," Mother said. "Keep the secret, and don't give the British any reason to suspect us."

"Could I just tell Andrew?" Brian asked. "To prove we aren't Tories."

"No one," Mother said firmly.

"After we win?" Brian asked.

"Then you may tell the entire city of Philadelphia."

"I hope it won't be long," Brian said.

"Rob told me that if the French join us, the war will end soon," Annie said.

They did not have to wait long for good news. By month's end, Benjamin Franklin, Philadelphia's most famous citizen, signed a treaty with

France. French ships would soon sail for the colonies, bringing the help that Washington needed.

Not long after, Mother whispered to Annie, "General Howe is leaving Philadelphia."

"That means we won't have to put up with these officers any longer," Annie said.

"No, they're staying, but with a new commander. General Howe was replaced. They say it's because he kept his soldiers here all winter instead of going out to fight Washington."

"Ha," Annie said. "Then I'm glad we made things so comfortable for them."

The British finally left Philadelphia in June, never to return. By that time, Washington's army was ready to fight. Even though the war did not end for three more years, Annie and her family had no doubt who would win. The Liberty Bell in Philadelphia rang out with the news of Washington's victory at Yorktown in 1781. And then, Brian did try to tell everyone in Philadelphia what his sister had done to win the war.

Nine years later, Annie saw Washington again. He had just been elected President of the United States. Philadelphia's people lined the streets to cheer him as he rode through the city. Annie and her family watched from the second-story windows of their house. On his white horse, Washington looked just the same as he had at Valley Forge.

"Hooray for President Washington!" Annie shouted. He looked up and saw her, and then saluted. Perhaps it was because he saw the sign MacDougal Fine Cloth with his picture on it, which Mr. Brent had added after the war. But in her heart Annie knew that Washington remembered the little girl who had been his spy.

MAKING A
SILHOUETTE

DRAWING an outline of a shadow was perhaps the earliest form of art. Scientists think that some of the cave paintings done by prehistoric people may have been done that way.

However, in the 18th century, making silhouettes became a popular fad in both Europe and the American colonies. The name itself comes from a French finance minister, Etienne de Silhouette. His hobby was making shadow likenesses of his friends. When the idea spread, people called these shadow-pictures "silhou-ettes."

Some silhouettes were very elaborate. Artists began to draw full-length miniature figures, complete with scenery such as grass, trees, and flowers. These pictures were often mounted and framed.

Materials Needed

Sheet of white paper at least $11'' \times 14''$ in size, Tape, Dark black pencil (a charcoal drawing stick would be helpful), Scissors, Lamp (the best kind would be one that can be aimed sideways.)

Steps

1. Have a friend or relative sit sideways next to a wall. They should be fairly close to the wall so that their shadow will not be too large.
2. Aim the lamp so that it throws the shadow of the subject's head onto the wall.
3. Tape the sheet of paper over the shadow. (Don't do this on wallpaper or any kind of wall that tape would damage.)
4. Darken the room to make the shadow as clear as possible.

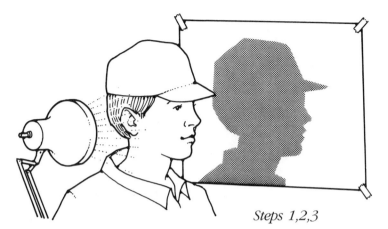

Steps 1,2,3

5. Ask your subject to sit very still.
6. Trace the outline of the shadow onto the paper.
7. Fill in the outline with pencil or charcoal.

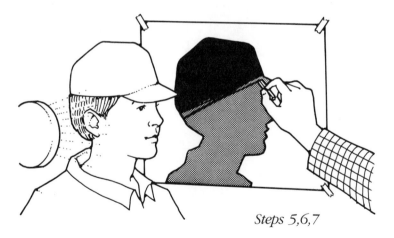

Steps 5,6,7

Instead of step 7, you can cut out the white-paper outline of the shadow. Then place it over a sheet of black paper, and cut around the outline to make a black silhouette. Then paste the black paper onto a thick piece of white cardboard.

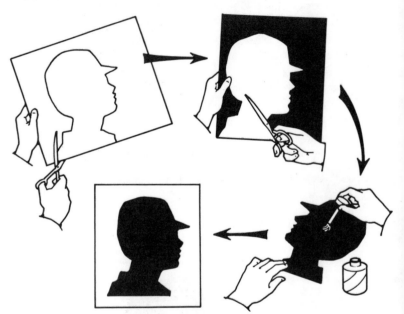

Tips

Be especially careful in tracing the shape of the nose, lips, and hair. This will help to make a clear likeness of the person.

The silhouette may be more interesting if you have the person wear something like a hair ribbon or baseball cap.

ADDITIONAL TITLES AVAILABLE
IN THE **HER STORY** SERIES,

by Dorothy and Thomas Hoobler:

Read the story of . . .

Sarah Tsaluh Rogers in
The Trail on Which They Wept:
The Story of a Cherokee Girl
By Hoobler & Hoobler/Burrus
LSB 0-382-24331-5
jh/c 0-382-24333-1
s/c 0-382-24353-6

Amy Elizabeth Harris in
Treasure in the Stream:
The Story of a Gold Rush Girl
By Hoobler & Hoobler/Carpenter
LSB 0-382-24144-4
jh/c 0-382-24151-7
s/c 0-382-24346-3

Maria Hernandez in
A Promise at the Alamo:
The Story of a Texas Girl
By Hoobler & Hoobler/Hewitson
LSB 0-382-24147-9
jh/c 0-382-24154-1
s/c 0-382-24352-8

Annie Laurie MacDougal in
The Sign Painter's Secret:
The Story of a Revolutionary Girl
By Hoobler & Hoobler/Ayers
LSB 0-382-24143-6
jh/c 0-382-24150-9
s/c 0-382-24345-5

Fran Parker in
And Now,
a Word from our Sponsor:
The Story of a Roaring '20's Girl
By Hoobler & Hoobler/Leer
LSB 0-382-24146-0
jh/c 0-382-24153-3
s/c 0-382-24350-1

Emily in
Next Stop, Freedom:
The Story of a Slave Girl
By Hoobler & Hoobler/Hanna
LSB 0-382-24145-2
jh/c 0-382-24152-5
s/c 0-382-24347-1

Laura Ann Barnes in
Aloha Means Come Back:
The Story of a World War II Girl
By Hoobler & Hoobler/Bleck
LSB 0-382-24148-7
jh/c 0-382-24156-8
s/c 0-382-24349-8

Christina Ricci in
Summer of Dreams:
The Story of a World's Fair Girl
By Hoobler & Hoobler/Graef
LSB 0-382-24332-3
jh/c 0-382-24335-8
s/c 0-382-24354-4

"This is a well-written and informative series with believable characters."
— American Bookseller "Pick of the Lists"

For price information or to place an order, call toll-free 1-800-848-9500.

Kingsway Christian Church / School

WD

Fic
Hoobler

HOOBLER
The Sign Painter's Secret

DATE DUE

KINGSWAY
CHRISTIAN
SCHOOL
LIBRARY